T0146903

The Smart Kid

The Smart Kid

Minister Evelyn Anderson

Rev. date: 12/17/2014

To order additional copies of this book, contact:
Xlibris
1-888-795-4274
www.Xlibris.com
Orders@Xlibris.com
700936

Dedication

THIS BOOK IS DEDICATED TO THE
UNBELIEVERS! NO MATTER IF YOU
BELIEVE THE BIBLE OR NOT, YOUR
TIME IS WINDING DOWN ON THIS
EARTH, SO HOW DO YOU WANT TO
BE VIEWED OR WHAT MEMORIES
WILL YOU BE LEAVING BEHIND.....
DON'T TAKE TOO LONG TO THINK
ABOUT THE SITUATION BECAUSE THE
NEXT MINUTE ISN'T PROMISED TO
ANYONE!!! – (Minister Evelyn Anderson)

This book is dedicated to the world of innocent kids that's been manipulated by an adult at one time in their life I'm reaching out to tell every child that it's not always your fault kids don't ask for certain parents they have to accept the guardian that's provided to them keep your head up better days are ahead of you..

This child like many other respected his

guardian and fell into a mind frame that

could get him locked away being incarcerated

could be his nightmare unless life chooses

to bless him while doing wrong let's try

to understand the mind frame of this

child as everyday is dictated to him but

how could that be. Yet being the smartest

kid at school is great well. Time reveals

all things come go with this child as he

discover who or what's going on in his life.

In this story we will read about a

junior high school kid, named Leroy,

yet some called him The Smart Kid

because of the Straight (A's) that he

earned. A special group of boys wanted

to socialize with Leroy, but he didn't

have time for those receiving failing

grades. While Leroy was busy trying to

avoid this special group of boys, others

wanted to know what was happening

at his home and the school campus.

This book allows a situation to be viewed in different angles, yet as children of God we are blessed because God watches over us. We sometimes can feel angels around us, have you read the poetry "*foot prints in the sand*?" It's similar.

"Resources"

Hebrew 1:14, Angels are God's messengers, spiritual beings created by God and under his authority (Colossians 1:16). They have several functions: serving believers (1:14), **protecting** the helpless (Matthew 18:10), proclaiming **God's messages (Revelation 14:6-12) and executing God's judgment.** (Acts 12:1-23; Revelation 20:1-3).

Gn. 16:7   Ex 23:20   Jdgs. 2:1

2 Sm 24:16   1 Kgs 19:7   2 Kgs 19:35

Hos 12:4......He struggled with the angel.......

Acts 12:7......Suddenly an angel of the Lord......

Life Application Study Bible
(NEW INTERNATIONAL VERSION)
PUBLISHED BY: Tyndale
House Publishers, Inc.

Wheaton, Illinois

AND

Zondervan Publishing House
Grand Rapids, Michigan

The Smart Kid

The first day of school started to approach, as usual the children went shopping for school clothes. Leroy didn't have to worry about going school shopping because his Uncle did it for him as long as Leroy continued to get good grades.

It was the first day of school and everyone looked nice with their hair styling and profiling. You could smell the new paint on the campus walls and it seemed like everyone had on a new pair of shoes. Leroy counted over 50 shoes that looked new but he stopped counting when he heard his name being called.

As he looked up he saw kids from last year who were annoying and they thought they knew it all. As Leroy walked away the boys continued to follow him, so he quickly turned around to ask what they wanted. The boys said, "hang with us this year," but instead of agreeing to it, Leroy said, "you guys are nothing but trouble," then turned and walked away. Shocked by his response they walked in the other direction but not before saying, "what did we do to him?"

During class time Leroy volunteered to assist the teacher with grading papers when each test was completed. After all of the tests were completed and turned in, he placed happy faces on passing tests and sad faces on failed tests. Since Leroy was last to leave the classroom he decided to change a few grades in the teacher's grade book before going home. All the way home he laughed and talked out loud to his self, saying, "Those annoying boys will surely stop and get out of my way, if it's the last thing I do!" As Leroy walked down the street, people cleared the path and moved away from him, but it did not bother him.

Instead he continued his journey home and ignored the boys club when they tried to invite him to their social book club. When Leroy finally reached his uncle's house he ate dinner, then showered and went right to bed. The next morning when Leroy woke up, he decided that he'd rather ride his bike to school instead of walk today. As soon as he made it to school he quickly put his bike in the bike rack, then went straight to class.

While walking to class Leroy saw the boys from the boys club and they were glad to see Leroy. They congratulated him on the test but instead of saying thank you, he asked the boys "how did you know my grade" They said, "It was posted on the bulletin board under THE SMART KIDS section." The boys then handed Leroy a bottle of water then one kid said, "Can you study with us and help us with our homework?" Leroy started running to class but slowed down when he saw how upset the other students were. He did not care because he saw the graded tests on his desk with an A+.

While the other kids stood in the hallway whispering, Leroy listened to the teacher talking saying, "all those who failed the lesson return to class!" All the students returned back to class except for Leroy, he got his bike and off he went. When he got home he watched television, then showered then he went right to sleep.

Leroy woke up early the next morning thinking about upcoming finals, at school next week. He walked to his Uncle's room and knocked on the door; as soon as his uncle came to the door, Leroy quickly said, "finals are next week and I need to study." his uncle lifted Leroy's chin so that they were staring eye to eye and said, "Don't waste your time in that book, just go to school." So Leroy obeyed his orders, he said good bye then turned and went to school.

Class was nice, they watched a film instead of doing school work, because it was a rainy day. The teacher asked Leroy to stamp the graded papers and pass them out to the students. When the film was over, everyone got upset after they saw the grades that they received from the assignment. All the boys from the boys club failed the assignment again, so when the bell rang Leroy left like always, but this time the teacher caught up with Leroy in the hallway.

Leroy turned when he heard the teacher call his name and saw her smiling at him. She said, "If I could have more students like you I could rest a little more." "All your papers since the beginning of school are great, an A+ or B, just keep up the good work, you're a smart kid," Then she smiled again, turned and returned to the classroom.

Leroy had the whole weekend to study, instead his uncle taught him how to build a tree house. On Saturday night Leroy slept up in the tree house and all he could hear was the birds chirping all night long. Later that evening, Leroy closed the tree house door and it got jammed. He tried pulling the door closed when he saw a shadow pass below the tree house near the ground! When he looked down he got angry and began to yell, "Get off my property losers."

The 3 boys from the boys club were standing near the tree house and one of the boys said, "What a nice tree house can we come up there and study with you?"

"No! No! Shouted Leroy. "How did you get on my property?" The three boys said, "If you could help us just once we'll leave you alone." Leroy yelled for his uncle, "Uncle please help me!" Within 2 minutes his uncle came running through the yard. Leroy yelled at his uncle, "Why did you let them get away."

His uncle stood there confused and said, "Let who get away?" Leroy replied by saying, "Those boys from my school that just ran passed you." "There was no one in this yard but us, all the gates are locked and the security cameras are on, just go to sleep Leroy! That dust from the wood must have made you see things." The uncle went back into the house and into his small room, then silently locked the door. After the incident, Leroy scratched his head then returned inside the tree house without any problems with the door.

Falling to sleep was easy because he had a busy day building that tree house and his body was tired, so he went back to sleep. As he rode his bike to school the next morning, he knew this was the biggest day of the year, relating to knowledge in groups or individuals. It was the quiz for the spelling contest, in which the school assigned students from different schools to participate in the contest. The spelling words were beyond their age groups and the students had to have knowledge of them as well as pass the test to be in the contest.

Now, Leroy has went two years in a row with straight A's and he has won different contests at the Jr. High School he's attending. Even the smart kids from each school that read about him identified him as the smart kid. When Leroy entered the gates at school all the kids made way for him; laughing, smiling and trying to be friends with him. He kept his head up and walked right passed all of them as if they didn't even exist. Leroy knew he was going to win the contest because his mentality was that he was the only smart kid on the earth.

The auditorium was crowded, but that made Leroy more confident. He felt like the more people, the better for him because his name would spread around town and everyone would know he was The Smart Kid. As the students and the judges took their seats, everyone then stood for the pledge of allegiance and singing of a song, then everyone was seated. The judges introduced each student and the school they were attending followed by a short speech about the student. Starting with Leroy the judge said, "Leroy Brown, age 12, was born and raised here in Houston Texas.

He's an 8th grader who has earned over 200 credits to graduate from 9th grade and he's currently in the 8th grade. Leroy's spelling and mathematics tests were graded as an A+ and he has had perfect attendance for 2 consecutive school years. He has never went home early for sickness or illness nor any other emergency. He has never attended after school or online studies, yet he has earned his name and those who know him will also agree. So let everyone stand and welcome Leroy Brown, better known as THE SMART KID!

Instead of standing and thanking the audience like the rest of Leroy's peers would do; Leroy stood and took a bow then sat back down. All the students had a high chair at a table to match, with a big red button on the center of the table. When a question was asked, the first to answer the question by pushing the button then saying the correct answer got points. If the answer was wrong then points were deducted from them. The contest lasted for 2 hours and like always Leroy won the contest which now qualified him to go to the state finals in 6 months.

He was awarded a big blue ribbon with the contest name and date on it; it was awesome. So awesome that all the kids walked passed him just to look at his ribbon. When Leroy got to the bike rack, the boys from the boys club were standing there with a 6 pack of flavored water that had a ribbon on it. They said, "Hi smart kid! Here is our gift to you." Leroy replied by saying, "You can drink it I have plenty at home."

Then he rode off on his bike and rushed home to celebrate with his Uncle. When he got home, his uncle congratulated him by placing the biggest sign in front of his house that said, "I KNEW YOU COULD DO IT." So, like always he had dinner, watched TV, took a shower then off to the tree house he went. The next morning, Leroy climbed out of the treehouse and entered his uncle house, as he reached around his neck he noticed his glasses were nowhere to be found. Leroy's uncle gave him a new pair that he kept clean and ready for Leroy, then off to school he went.

This year something changed, Leroy saw someone at the grading table and the teacher said to the class "because this is the last test of the year we have the vice principal here to grade papers." Leroy was very upset because this wasn't the plan he had in mind. As he looked around the class he said, "these kids aren't going to pass anyways so can they be excused to go home." Of course that didn't happen. As the test was being taken the vice principal walked around the class with what looked like a walkie talkie or a small radio.

It strangely sent off sounds as he walked around the classroom, finally the sound was so loud that Leroy looked up and the principal was standing next to him. As Leroy started to look around the room, he realized he was being lifted out of his chair. Just then his glasses started beeping, so the teacher grabbed the glasses off Leroy's face and he was taken to the office. While examining the glasses they noticed a small microchip on both sides of his glasses. They also noticed that the lens received email from outside the class and they could hear someone talking on the mic to Leroy.

Within 30 minutes the police showed up at Leroy's uncle house and found him in a small room in the basement giving Leroy the answers to the test. The police arrested Leroy's uncle and he was immediately taken to jail.

As they escorted Leroy from school to the police car, one of the boys from the boys club shouted out loud and said, "Hey smart boy see

you next fall." Leroy said "no you won't you and your boys failed all the tests this year, but I passed."

The teacher walked up and said we have been watching you the whole year and we have you on video erasing the tests and now we have your glasses. This is all the evidence we needed, so Leroy you won't be coming back to graduate and the vice-principal is going to look over the paperwork from last year also!" As the kids crowded the stairway the officer rushed him away quickly and into the police car. Leroy could hear all the kids laughing and then as he turned around for 1 last look at the school the boys from the boys club were holding 3 signs that read GOD LOVES YOU...WE FORGIVE YOU and SEE YOU SOON.

He couldn't believe what he was reading, and all the way to jail he was quiet. When he finally spoke he asked the officers, "What is the name of the boys club?" Both officers smiled and said, "THE GUARDIAN ANGELS." When Leroy arrived at the County Police Department they booked him but later he was released to the child protective services. Once again he was riding in a government agency car, but this time he began crying. When he looked over at the Lady from children protective services he asked "what's going on? I was at school then arrested, where are you taking me lady."

She replied, "Before placing you in a group home, you have to be interviewed about your uncle." Upon arrival at the court building they entered the investigation room, where there was a court appointed attorney already waiting for Leroy to arrive. In the investigation room they informed Leroy that what his uncle had did was wrong and in conclusion, his uncle was arrested for misleading a minor, illegal equipment on school campus (glasses), stolen high price equipment and computers in home, and child neglect for 2 years and much more. "Your uncle will not be coming home for many years and you are to be placed in an emergency shelter if nothing permanent is found."

Leroy told the officers that his Uncle told him for the past few years that schooling was a waste of time and he wanted Leroy to enjoy life like a child should. The officer said to Leroy that after Leroy's parents passed away 3 years ago from a drunk driver accident he was the next of kin, so Leroy went home with Uncle Bobby. "Although, Bobby wasn't his real uncle, he had escaped prison 3 years ago and knew his parents so they introduced him to you as your uncle Bobby. Yet, Bobby had a name change, a facial change, and changed his lifestyle by hiding out in your parents' home trying to raise you.

We now have proof that he had something to do with your parent's death by tampering with the vehicle's brakes that failed. We found out that your Uncle Bobby was known to be their mechanic. A hurtful 2 hours went by and Leroy was tired, irritated and he felt alone, so he lowered his head on the table. That is when they concluded that the case was closed and emergency placement was ordered. One last time Leroy was placed in the Child Protective Service car with the social worker on their way to a group home.

As soon as they arrived at the group home Leroy quickly noticed the three boys from the boys club playing in the front yard. As he got out of the car they came up to Leroy and one of the boys said, "Told you that we would see you again." The second boy said "Everything's going to be okay, "then the third boy said, "You are going to love it here." Leroy walked to the front door with the social worker and they were greeted by a lady who asked them to come in.

Once they got inside Leroy asked the lady, "do the boys outside live here too?" She responded by saying, "what boys?" Leroy stood in silence looking at the social worker. The social worker then asked him, "Leroy, did you see boys outside?" The lady of the house said, "You are the only one here but let's take a look outside." As they all stood in the front door way, they looked out at the the vehicles in the driveway, but no boys were to be seen nor heard anywhere...

(ONLY LEROY COULD SEE THEM)

THE END!!!

The Authors Bio

Minister Evelyn Anderson was born in 1966 to the proud parents, Rev. William Anderson and Sister Rosie Lee Anderson of Long Beach, California. Living a Christian life was very becoming for her due to the fact that she had plenty of time to read, and yes, the closet was her number one spot to relax with the light on and read. Serving under different pastoral leadership has taught her to humble herself as a child would do, and that allowed Evelyn to put herself into a child's mind. Evelyn is known for her great love for people. She realizes that you can love the individual but not their ways. This is her second book available for the world to read.

Certifications Awards/Diploma

Desk Clerk

Certified Nurse's Aide

High School Diploma

Medical Administrative Assistant

License Foster Parent

Parents Participation

Teacher 1st & 2nd grader

Social Worker

EKG Technicians

Phlebotomist

Author

Licensed Minister............Gospel Crusade

Ministerial Fellowship

Website: *http://www.evelynbooks.biz*

Email: *hopefortomorrow1966@yahoo.com*

Evelyn Blog @ Weebly.com

Twitter @ Evelyn Nona

Contact # 951 956-0047

Availability resources

Amazon. Com

Barnes & Noble

Goodreads

BAM. .Books A Millions

Manta

Evelyn Blog @ Weebly.Com